POETICAL Renais

Dare To Arouse Your Sense of Desire

LISA CLARK

T0380371

To order additional copies of this book, contact:
Xlibris
844-714-8691
www.Xlibris.com
Orders@Xlibris.com

ISBN: Softcover   978-1-9845-3604-4
          EBook   978-1-9845-3605-1

Print information available on the last page

Rev. date: 01/12/2023

POETICAL
Renais

Dare To Arouse Your Sense of Desire

A romance on canvas

She lay motionless and beautiful in lace on satin sheets
Just like a Mona Lisa with a smile so sweet
Her elegance aroused me, her beauty caught my eyes
Her stillness made me lust for her all the time

She's the goddess of desire, Aphrodite is her name
The mother of pure romance, the princess of love games
A trickster and deceiver the mystery in your style
I don't know what you're thinking yet I'm truly driven wild

I love your special features in that perfect shade of light
And everything the artist did was in your best delight
A picture I admire, she's a person I embrace
My feelings I so desire, a lifestyle that I crave

My Mona Lisa work of art, my master peace of grace
My charming rose, jasmine scent and eyes as green as jade
I want you and I mean this, you make me stand real tall
And that is why I love to have this picture on my wall

By Lisa Clark

Blue Rose

A blue rose makes a whisper for you
A lullaby's sweet in the rainbow so true
I listened attentive and ponder this charm
The sweet sensations tingles my warm
It stung me light like each dandy of stars

I absorbed crystal moments like the flowing streams
Romance out of nowhere that's tainted my dreams
Reality so tempting captivates this blinkers life
Joyful praise, pleasure some pain, a tinker bell chime
A feeling never ending that's centered around time

Play me hot like wild bluebells so sensual
Catapulted with lust you radiates and bloom
Craved by your touch I'm blest with your sex
This poised each feeling, I painted your image
This sexual caption melts our neutron of chemistry

By Lisa Clark

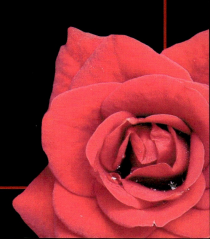

Blueberry Delights

I nibbled a blueberry, fruity and delicious
I pampered sweet succulence, luscious so warm
I stroke its very juicy delight with my lips
I tended this blueberry of nestle and cream

I feast so precious, I romp with pleasure
The natured contents so palpable on my tongue
I redeem each joy, a candy of pure lust
Smothering this delicate taste untold

I pondered, so warm in my mischief thoughts
Beauty personified your wanton passion
My blueberry resembled your rippled sexuality
Your awesome sexual cream flowing in fountains

Creates colors of the rainbow so brighten bloom
Enlightening my beams so wild and sexual
Proposing my dreams, you are mystery unfold
Feeding my needs to the fantasies of pure gold

By Lisa Clark

Candy Stranger

The night is wanton, the night is new
The night is parried, the winds blew cool
There swifts a female in her dent dark room
She grid her perfect upon her bed
Her eyes lay close she listens still

Her body is naked so wet from shower
Spades of droplets be dribbles down lower
Her window invites the warm night breeze
The wind it blow whence were it pleased
The moon shone thru the thick black amaze

The gives of it, a chorded phase
Distinct symphonies, kettered from splints
The volume in fades, here falls to its lift
Drifted she tries, with sleep all filled
The concord of music took her thrill

Enjoy its melody, the sparks of a symphony
She heard the silence rattles in slow
She hears him enter, the dark tranquil room
Once then was gone, hence now its new
A love once was gone, its back to bloom
The night drew fast, the time drum still
The lure of lust, he's come at will
She feels his hand brazed her breast
He brought with him candies for zest

His piercing eyes read through her mind
The looks of love, he braced his time
The flower of passion, he wants the wreath
Her tender caress he's summon her dream
He open her thighs, to fashion his nest
His fingers enjoy, they teased and test
He tended each moments, to feel her needs
Addictive he savoured to hears her pleas

Her body sublimes to his sexual clench
She wants him madly, his cock beseech
She sievers their playtime she wait, and waits
There less than lame his truce will claim

Arrive are the moments she wicker oblige
To feel his thick cock inside her crave
Steadied his body, he throb and push
His thick huge cock inside her lush

Wetting her with cum juice, he fucks her to the core
Pulling her to ecstasy, he delved in deeper
Two bodies pant sexual, inside their fitted minds
Soft Slides and slithers, his slow sweet fuck play

He spurred on each daring, watching her beg
Each cloven of moment peaks them higher

his cock dance inside her tighten cunt

and fucks her even more

Chad's Lair

Prologue: I like my breast sucked, tucked and fucked

Prince of my fire, true prince of my reign
A diamonds lux gift, an amethyst of grace
Tasting his pleasures, I captured each phase
His stars shine bliss, and fiery neon's blaze

His spirit proves pleasing, his treasure so charmed
He held me perfect delicious and tasty, ever so warm
We cherished momentums, we blazoned and sweat
He supple my ripples, he fucked me so wet

We dared not finito, we comprehend surpass
We blessed each notion, we showered each cast
My prince of fire had sure ruptured my mass
He fucked me senseless, and tantalized our dance

My grip held strong, so firm and levered
As juices of cum spewed and spilled over
I lectured his juice each lull of my tongue
I lapped all his milk, ere so I was done

His groans belled strong, pressure rush high
I listened his plateaux he blest my sweet ride
Sex crazed we festered, we cared not second best
And rested we did, awaits our second test

By Lisa Clark

Charms

How strong do you feel when you thought of her
How hard do you stir when visualized her sweet
How long did you steer to redeem her flesh
How sweet are the desires dare ponder her test

The tender solace of your love held her firm
Close your eyes to experience the joys of fantasy
Your swims of naughtiness sheared her desires
Sexually flavored, your strokes fill her G

Your fashionable wetness ignites her fire
Desires of each precious moments she feels
Your grinding rhythms tortured her passions
You melted in her like hot buttery cream

She tasted your tongue the flavor of strawberry
You ate her lips as you stroke her deeper
You sought me fully, delicious with softness
Taking her slowly, enchants her to the full

By Lisa Clark

Chocolate Bar

You are chocolate melting caramel on her lips
Sweet honey suckled lemon drops tingled her tits
Crispy crunching almond, she tastes your delight
Your peach dips with lave whipped cream
Nectarine fruit to flavored your exotic taste

Your sensual enchantment gyrated her thoughts
Pleasing warm enticing me hot and powerful
The pleasures of passion control in her mind
Ascending her pressure to its fullest capacity
Fucking her deep you throb her wild

You engulf her flames with rhythms of passions
Prophecying your love, foretelling each mystery
Though thoughtful you are, and bright you seem
The philosophy of your nectar filling in her

By Lisa Clark

Chocolate Confetti

I sucked on a confetti caramel toffee
Delicious milk in hot chocolate, tantalized me
I savored its clammy juices daringly wet
The aroma scented, it's flavored so sensual
So purged and purify the delicacy of me

My taste bud enjoyed this confetti of milk
The melting juicy droplets caressed my heat
My thoughts remembered thy sexual sweetness
Naughty pleasured semen, clammy and creamed
Purged my thirsty tongue tasty and true
Purified, my passions glorified in ecstasy

By Lisa Clark

Comely Lover

How delicious do you feel stroking her core
How pleasant it feels when she taste the moments
Currents of your selected pleasure hot in pursuit
Electrifying and magical, you drove her wild

Sweet succulent are your rhythms peaks her wetness
She close her eyes as your pacing strokes threw higher
The feel of your sexuality craved you for more
The strength of your palms caressed her nipples

The warmth of your lips arousing her desires
The tender peace of your kisses played her neck
How provocative are the nature of your passions
The lustful charms of your love juices within her

Caress her with the thoughts of your emotions
Fondle her with the gentle tips of your fingers
Slithers in her the tenders of your sexual toy
Magical, comely enjoying you forever

By Lisa Clark

Concerto Sexuale

A spade of truce, the king at hearts
A spade of love this moments last
A tingled joy in the paraded of gifts
My concerto dance in this grace of bliss

My doctored prince la luned so grand
His king at heart blossomed so strong
His thoughts are stir, he closed his eyes
His deeds are spun with notes a sigh

His sparkled jest, his sensual taste
He called me ere to fulfil her place
This pondered truth, not so in vain
An invitation, aught a secret so plain

I levelled my depth, I staton with care
I tallied my grim most ever sincere
He massage me awe, the beau of trust
I proven his phase this whisperer of lust

He bids O come before breaks of morn
His whispers of love to me so strong
I richly emblem his castle of praise
I regal empowered my galahad's jade

We flowered a kiss, a chemistry unplugged
We caught this momentum in concerto's lust
His voice is breathless, he craved for more
His adrenaline rush, away and doth and soar

He meddled his fingers upon my breast
He fondle my thighs, he natured his best
His cock is warm, our bodies spoke loud
A plateaux pleas phase a concept so proud

His speechless zeal to me his quest
I cautioned my heart it told me the rest
Concerto spoke true this prism of light
Sexuale my geste jon candi et une delite'

His cock so throbbed with sexual haste
He felt each pressure analyed its phase
And fantasy took hold of his sensual thought
An ecstatical rupture so pleasantly bought

He teased me high blueberries cascade
He enters me hot, so sated and suede
His mesmerized fuck, it capture a taste
Our entourage of love with silken lace

He lulled my ears and nibbled my neck
His fucks are tasty our bodies did sweat
His whispers of satin my moments respond
His twinkles of diamond pristinely bond

He hugged me closed in a breath of dais
His caption of heart rang soft note blaise
He sprinkles with tinkles in kisses of blu
His spangled of toffee with delicious anew

He smiles with his lips brightly displayed
He measured his heart with options relayed
This joyous forth bring and gladly he states
This ultra of tenders this love has create

By Lisa Clark

Cream of Ecstasy

I lay calm with tenderness, peaceful and still
So mild in my slumber, my thoughts I did fill
My body is naked, its hot, wet and warm
My beauty stood supple, slippery so swarm

My nipples felt delicate erect for a taste
My lover, he had them savouring each pace
He fondle and tickled and pucker his ploy
He suckle their sweetness fulfilling his joy

He made me naughty, warm and caressing
As his fingers wet with juices now enlightens
He part my thigh ready nurturing my maze
He position my projection to prosper his haste

I felt his thick cock inside my core
I felt each ripple and begging for more
His sex is slow paced, grind me with ease
His cock is delicious, he made me scream

He shove, fuck and freak me right through
His palms stir my hips so levered so hue
His sex tallied long and whipped pure pace
Our passions of sweat beads wet of lace

By Lisa Clark

Delicious Diamonds

Delicious essence you are the beauty of roses
Diamonds hast fill your being in the sweep of laughter
Emeralds glow like a ray of sunlight upon you
In thy countenance sweet fury became your captive

Amethyst sprinkled and sprayed at your feet compacted
As I remember your honest passions hot and sexual
Soft and smooth taboos exploded in fantasies
Your caress, so warm and tender is what we shared

My thoughts pondered me that you crave for more
My darling ecstatic lover, hold my hand forever
Treasure me in your dreams, aroused in your heart
Behold, my firm nipples in your nectar thoughts

Behold, your passion inside me deep
Your hot throbbing cock, swell and sweet
Your spills of juices lulled on my tongue
Delicious dare diamond, you are my one
Wandering, roaming, luscious and free
Delicious dream diamonds, you aught to be

By Lisa Clark

Erotic : Love ode: Male's longing embrace for his Female

Just as high tides splashes the rock and foams away
So does his passions is desirous to posses her
Will his eyes again behold the flower he's long to hold
She wanders and roams within the patterns of his thoughts
Her charming ebbs and flow untangles his dying heart
His emotions races to the boundaries that captivate her
Pulling each catapulted bond, their chemistry sheer divinity
He touch her delicate flesh, the pressure is too much
Feeling this erotic ecstasy, glistens like wet dew
The hot peppered warmness, slimed in friction
This daring sexuality he enjoyed inside her pure lush
Emotionally creating us, rhythmatically fusing them
And sexually uniting them in this cast forever

By Lisa Clark

Fellatio Sexual

Nurturing her taste his lollipop with cum
She suckled his moments ere she was done
Erect was his cock she stroke him forthwith
She auctioned each ripples, this dame she is swift

She puckered and press and pampered and played
This daring her task, she swindled and swayed
Her moans were pleasures, she tottered his glans
With her fingers she lave him between her tits

He played upon her dandy, he prick, he played, he shoved
He cleave his cock supple forthwith, inside her he had cum
She scream and grip his torso, she perfected his grasp
She glued her body unto his, their sex was meant to last

Their treasures are forbidden spangled jewels gems
Their apple of naked clustered, erotic scenes adrift
Strawberry cream and lemon pie took them where they went
To their never ending mystery from heaven she must be sent

By Lisa Clark

Forever Mine

I captioned, I swayed with deems of grace so dear to me
I captioned, I prayed for the one who stole my heart to him
I closed my eyes each day and pray a song for him
A delicious momentum for the grace he paved
What beauty he held and such laughter he gave
What diamond he sprinkled, bright rainbows glowing
The beauty in his eyes held me in sweet captive
A story unraveled of untold eons and centuries
The laughter in him held firm and daring with legerity

I tasted his kisses so delicious, so sensual, so awesome
I praised him for joys he brought my redeem austerity

With everything proposed for my dearly beloved
With everything he has given me, I have tasted him true
I have showered him with lux of blessings nesting as lilies
I can only say this once and forever many more
Je t'aime Raj Ra Chadr' with all dears of my generosity

By Lisa Clark

Her Secret Admirer

His eyes of ocean... becomes captivated
All proposed in the captions of splendor
He stand across the dance floor, so grand
Standing tall with the regents so dignified
The smooth roughness of his palms

So huge, sensual, so... !...wet
Caressed the crystal wine filled glass,
His eyes, they danced and twinkled
In the glimmers spangled of light
His pure Italian countenance, all a glow
Dance in the beautiful dandy lights

His smile captured in authentic of her dreams
And bewilders the thrashing aura of her esteems
The soft smoothness of his gentle Italian lips
Echoed in his velvets of sexual laughter

The warm champagne melting his lips
The sweetness stirred her erotic beams
Oh! her sensual sir, her secret admirer
He swept their thoughts, this secrecy of love
That phases them, that encircles, it bonds
Will thence unite them

By Lisa Clark

His Play Toy

What passion and naughty ecstasy she brought him
Savoring delicious taste of cream purifying her tongue
Flavoring the warm wet pressure throbbing her deep
Craving her, the need of his hot toffee purging her heat
Warm joy, naughty delicious pain sending desires

Blessing her with his heart, please her with his thoughts
Pleasure him with her flesh, inviting his passions
Nature is spontaneous, wild hot sexual dilemnas
He created true fantasies beyond her wildest dreams
And melt her being with his hot thickness

He tasted aphrodisiac thorn in her flesh
The sensual warmth caressing her delicate babe
She postured and sway from the darts of cupid
Their lust of sexual heat took to the celestials
Touching the magical mystics from beams of the sun

By Lisa Clark

His Sexual Essence

Delicious and luscious, he tasted her dreams
Wanting and waiting to savour her needs
Delightful and dazzling softly his redeem
Precious and pleasing the more she seem

She's painted and pretty an angel so bright
She is fragile and tender a spangle of delight
Ivory of caramel, her fiery sexual tone
Beauty of butter she radiantly shone

Her eyes are bronze and fragments of oak
Her lips smile in whisper and delicate they spoke
He touched her sweet hence licking her warm
She opened for him, her essence so form

His vixen of Mona, his enchanted aura
An honor so sexual, in perfect appraised
His embrace to dress her yearning need
She sexually pleads sweet faith is his cream

By Lisa Clark

Hot Fuck

Bubbly so juicy, delicious and nice
Lovers so luscious, in tempting his heights
Softly so beautiful, this night to play dames
Sultry and sexy, the prince of sex games

A knightly armored camest oh! He did
Hot with desires and passions blend heat
I truce myself, I endorsed my thoughts
I regard my conscious, I praise my cause

I entered with ease his regent décor
Etched closer to him, he slammed the door
Drowning for sex, his tensions roar high
Jelled with emotions in the cool pure night

He fashioned to chef his kitchenly delights
Haa!! I tasted cuisine of splendid delights
Color crone candles ambiances the room
Yellow, pink and orange all flicker around

My mesmerized thoughts displayed aloud
He tippytoed behind me to display his shroud
He massage my shoulders, he fondled my tits
He whispered in my ears and kiss my neck

His passions endorsed and secrets amazed
He spun me fast, his twinkles so craved
Hot kisses found us, we redeem our lips
The warm blazing fire inside our hot grip

He heave sheets of spasm and moments do pause
He'd swiftly lie me down in seconds do wrought
Hot lightning was he, his redeem pulse of cock
He brazed his hands betwixt my sap set ready for fuck fete

His glans teased first my swell sap clit
He hypnotized my switch and enters bit by bit
He's now well groom the more of me
The need of chocolate we both ensuite

His strokes begins with slow reel pace
I dwindled sweet candies of my chaste
His strokes ebb stronger more his claim
He threw my ripples in each parallel plain

He whispered sensations in my ear
And fucked me wild hot to drum my dares
He pinned me tight on the silken sheets
While his swollen dick opt charge my heat

By Lisa Clark

Hot, wet and wild

Make hot sex to me and drown me with wet fuck
Freak me until you feel the pressure tingling of stars
O baby do me until your stiff cock throb and swell
Spangle my heat and fuck me long and wet

Feed your palms all over my body, so sensitizing
Thrust your fingers deep inside my supple softness
Work them forth and delicate, o numb my cradle
Make me clammy from the springs of your wetness

I bid you sweetly with the warmth of my fantasies
You are that calm and noble Galahad caressing my pink
You are that placid angel taking me to the highest peak
Circle me with the magic of sexuality, a masterpiece we are

Arouse me with ecstasy, the need of your delightful dick
Twinkle your hand over my nipples, play my aerolas gently
Take me to the brink of orgasm, fountains of juices melting in me
Pleasing wild, do me high, turn my table of passionate desires

By Lisa Clark

Jewel Lovers

The authenticity of our fuck took us whence wild and true
These golden aspirations catapulted our passions anew
He engaged her time hence bandwidth exchange
He spoke with blue qualms with regents of a duke

He thrush this quiet dare conceptually blest
He whispered this moment, putting her to the test
His words of gold tremors enlightens each quest
They stung her like stars in the blinkers of zest

He carefully took her to the satin sheer sheets
He lay her so tender on the warmth of satin beads
She felt her echo melted when he kissed her lips
His sweet trembled fingers caressed her swift

And next his lust lips found her soft neck
He romp and sucked and lulled and played
By this each crevice cramped her crave
Small whimpers of tone so drone his name

This heat of his body saturates her thoughts
The heat of his nestle milked her so hot
Locks them in fusion crowning their phase
Redemption of pleasures so beautifully laced

The moments are precious with sexual plaque around
Jewel lovers so held hearts in mysteries bound
And candlelight ambiances fill the sweet breathe air
Their truest love jewels shines so gleaming clear

By Lisa Clark

Kamadeva (Seducer of passions)

His soul is calm, rendered and poised
His laughter echoed in a whispering dream
His beauty shines like rays from the sun
His persona imposters the radiance of nature

His fuck is true and sweet as honey
Dipped in nectar ready to be savoured
Like soft white roses so pure in austerity
The beauty of his stride guided the swift river
He is her sunshine laughter on a rainy day

His smile ripens the perfection of day
He's Kamadeva, seducer of many passions
Feasting in her wet flesh, tasting her cream
Savoring her drip flavor warm and redeem

By Lisa Clark

Kiss

A taste of crème as pure as the rain
A taste so sweet that whispers her name
A trend that last to blend each stir
As trends of truce to mesmerized her

Sweet darling of lust this remnant of lust
Sweet darling his daze to have her he must
And thence her heart he captured her maze
The times of thoughts in their fiery blaze

He rode the winds in the twilight of skies
His carpet dost carried him seemingly high
His thoughts engraved on her beautiful face
He thought of her physique so sensual of lace

His beams set twinkled her tottered of taste
Enlightened like rainbow color treasured chest
He touched the sands of purified blest twinks
The home of his favored, his dream to meet

And there she stood she awaits his vows
She solemnly greets with a cast and bow
Beauty spoke true in her smiling bromade
She daringly hugged his propelled encase

A message was sent, their eyes met affixed
This message of bond their chemistry doest mix
He tasted her lips, her perfections of delight
He tasted it well in the dark hems of night

By Lisa Clark

Lollipop Cream

Tasty, sweet, his wet lollipop with cream
Full to the flavor and cocks in delight
She sucks in the juices, dripping, supple
He arouse her thoughts, nurturing her cunt

He fucks her wild, danced in her flesh
He slide, insatiable in and out her hotness
His pleasure is hers, his cock is wet
Caressing the need for his spontaneous love

Giving her lux of passions, blue lightning he see
She's lulling his toy and teasing him hot
To soar his desires to the brink of ecstasy
He kissed her lips, licking delicious lollipop juices

He tasted her tongue flavored with cream
Fondling the austerity of her nipples
The feel and firmness ere his treaded
His throb cock brush against her thighs

Inviting her in, craving his body for more
Love is hot, fucking her with diamond desires
Appealing her for more of him struttng her
His lover, his life, her forever him

By Lisa Clark

Love Unchanged

A splashing ocean, a roaring sea
Sings his symphony, our love is free
I felt his thought bleeding through me
His notional concepts raptures slowly

He is far away o'er the castile lands
His soul breathes short, to reach my hand
He toss each day, kept watch for time
He ponders my love, yet still he's mine

The days lapse near, to redeem my face
To feel my touch, it's wondrous grace
He knows no sleep, he cursed at slumber
He view my cosmic, like his world has crumble

Tho Pace of days have toll their time
My love, my prince has finally arrive
He touched my flesh, so ripe as honey
And fill my loins, my days are sunny

By Lisa Clark

Lovers Web

Fondling the concepts of her jetted thoughts
Bringing her sweet ecstasy thus employ
Touch her gently with the tip of his tongue
Caress her will, tenact the honesty of his love

Tracing his thick cock down her chest
Pleasure her heat with his ecstatic implore
Entrapping her in the web of his desires
Enfold her in the crest of his sexuality

Colors of rainbows encircle her beauty
Prism of stars nourished my heavens
Lulling her cunt with the spark of his sensuality
Enlighten her in the mystics of his lure

By Lisa Clark

Lustful Passions

A ray of hope with blessings delight
A twinkling star in the bliss twilight
The clouds are warm, the moon wax bright
An angel rode in the heavenly night

Her hair shone bright with ginger oak
Her skin tone fair so cleanly coat
Her lips gave joy to rubies untold
Her eyes of hazel with beauty they glow

He watched her dance the dark lit skies
Her smile so enticing, she's a pleasurable prize
She captured his stare, soft looks of lust
He will feast on her flesh, his dick he will thrust

She wavered and laughed, she held his hand
Soft musk was his scent, they in the sand
She opened for him to her tender of beam
As his stiff rod comfort her radiant dreams

By Lisa Clark

Midnight of Passions

An endless night, a passionate kiss
His beauty so charm, a treasure chest gift
An heavenly bliss this dark filled night
We centered our love to lift us high

The breeze trend calm, as nature stood still
My cupid of dreams enticed me his thrills
The bed was soft, the quills felt warm
Our chamber was dark; we were in for a storm

He kissed my lips and raked my fire
His fingers fondle my glows of desire
I twisted his tale to welcome his lust
He melted my wings inside me he'd thrust

His cock felt wet and warm for my cunt
He propel each stride to bring forth his cum
He fucked me with and tingle his stars
I moaned when his hjuices united our heart

By Lisa Clark

Passions Bliss

I have mystify your delightful of thoughts
I have perplex your mind in sweet ecstasy
I have cause you to mingle in sexual passion
I tinkled your sweet pain so sensually flavored
I have stirred your awe with blends of desire

I purged your heart and strike your soul
I dissipated your sexual heat soaring
I toy with your teddy so huge and luscious
I played with your cum warm with pleasure

I feel the ripples of your sexual throb
I felt your enchanted dick enticed my flesh
Your stroke ebb and flow, pulsate my warmness
And emptied your juices, semen of delight

By Lisa Clark

Perceptive Desires

The motivation of joy has captured the tendered vitality
And of my earliest passions, the times I had shared
With his handsome beauty and sweet sensuality
How can I forget the curves of such masculine figure
And the neatness of his form so carefully assembled
The succulence of his wetness revealing its sexual splendour
His fairness transpired the graceful calm all perfected
His complexion painted the brilliant colored caramel flower
With soft glowering so vividly of true amiable and blends
With the sweet precious that is more than convinced
I fell the warmth of his touch so grip my bewildered thoughts
The warm firmness of his breast so masculine ripen
The fullness of his pure fashion pleasing resistance

By Lisa Clark

Play Boy

Part my thighs and sexual nourishment shall be your joy
Run your fingers on my chest and feel me rising
Toy with my heat then taste the experience
Toy with my ripples and play with my lust

Make me hot, steamy and wild with passions
Drown me with wet sex, I feel your rhythms
Do me until your wetness pressure inside my heat
Feed me long and wet until I stir your senses

Touch my breast with your kissable lips
Toy me, tease me, play me entice me
Bright aural neon twinkling my stars
Wading me higher to this sexual peak

Each star you lit radiates my inner beams
Strike me with fresh fuck gyrated emotions
Send me to the highest pinnacle my play boy
Expulsions exploded you deep inside me

Expulsions so sexual creating these fantsies
Steamy hot juices warm, wet and provocative
Dark maze of new borne sexual ecstasies
Spinning our fuck fete to the newest track of rims

I love you, I dare this momentum fast and true
You took me with diamonds of sexual pristine
You tasted my pleasures, a fairy in its guise
Caressing and fondling your milk juices blend

By Lisa Clark

Pure Sex

You are hot, you are flavor wet
You are the grace inside a woman
I love your style, your plore of elegance
The feel of your roughness is authentic
And the blessing of your sexual cock
Throbs hard and wicked inside of me

You guised the swan's colorful pattern
Yet you dance betwixt my wet passion
With lace silk desires of your hot taste
Creating images of your fucks of ecstasy
You make me laugh, you make me scream
In the sweetness of your song you fucked me

You nurtured me with fucks of melted desires
You nibble my nipples, so fed them with your tongue
You teased my cunt with your craving fingers
"My lust, my love our bond is forever
The beauty of our song lingers on eternal

The pleasure of you toying delicious inside me
Your true spirited persona held my beams
Erotic.... so wet, rhythms...so wild, lust....so sensual
The taste of your hot, spilled juices lathers my tongue
My delicious pleasure of you, and always you

By Lisa Clark

Pyara

Mystical, precious handsomely creamed
His texture of caramel deliciously sweet
His piercing eyes twinkle like stars so bright
With lips so pure, he's cupid's knight

I captured his thoughts, he craved my soul
To savoir my wetness, his passions arose
I stroke his mind and entangled his need
Draining each motion, his sexual feed

I played him, with pleasures so strong
Delightful, I pleased his tempted twist
Entice my taste, his joy is mine
His fashion of beauty fathom entwine

His jovial aura portrays this lavender dove
His emotions of concepts tuned in for love
He's a rose encarved for lovely passions
He displays onyx prism of colorful bands
He is majestic, so stately dignified and tall

By Lisa Clark

Sex Games

He embraced her close in the strength of his arms
Nibbling the soft trueness of her lips
He brazed and kisses the tenders of her neck
While their bodies' peak to its sexual intensity

He stroke her hair, with the course of his fingers
He touched her cheeks, her inner soul tingle
She closed her eyes to savour his carnal dreams
She closed her thoughts and trapped him in

His tongue enjoyed the lustful pleasures of her tits
His palms carefully feasted the daring softness of her thighs
Enticingly warm was the wetness of his cock all prepared
Massing her wet labia, his sexual totter her dare

In the sweet prosperity she captured in glow
In their bright austerity she giggle with glee
The precious glitter of his delicious fuck
She moan at his berry fill delight in wonders

And so nurtured their wild fiery sexual games
As they dance did the metaphoric intensity of their love
Her beau tasted each ignited task endeared with power
Their wet naked love making will never be forgotten

By Lisa Clark

Sexual Glitters

Romance of caramel, tempted and subtle
Lulling flavours of Cadbury cream
Whip cream of passions filling my tables
Soft buttery icing melting my dreams

Like strawberry and cherries trickling my nipples
Dripping like wet butter, warm and sexual
Seeps down the contours of my palpable desires
Savour the hot delicate pleasures of my being

Make me your push pop wild and passionate
Make me your sultress a pupil of pleasure
Provoke me, predict to the fire of your heat
Invoke me; impress me to the glory of your test

Fruit phase of delight, my juices are wet
Peaches and nectarine waded my chest
Fleshy my pear sprinkling in glitters
Fill my hot wet beams to austere of your love

By Lisa Clark

Sexual Laced

Sexual lace it's wet joy untold
Amethyst of satin like sapphire's pure gold
Prisms of colours so radiant it shine
Prisms of you glorified my mind

Warm is his lull juice salty and sweet
Fed in my wetness, did me nicely
Hit me hard, straddle me tightly
Tingle my soul delicious and naughty

I tasted his cock and melt like chocolate
Delicate throbs fill my glorious peace
His semen of grace sprayed amidst
Inside my supple, inside me swift

By Lisa Clark

Sexual Mystiques

Hot with pressure, peppered sweet pain
Chocolate fudge in cream filling pie
I'm Strawberry apple I melt his brew
Berries of delight I savour his taste

Caramel cake soft and pudgy
Delicious desserts jelled his thoughts
Fountains of creams building like lava
A cherry amidst the palpable scene

Burst me wild with tenders of your sexual mystics
Gravitate me guy, and suckle me hot I scream
My Cadbury toy hence feeding me deep
He mystiques my mind, my lovable sweet

By Lisa Clark

Sexual Teddy Bear

Strike me with desires; entertains my zest
Prepare me for your sexual feast
Chew my lips, suck my tongue, taste my wet, until you're done
Teasing my neck, and kiss me all over

Please my nipple, fondle them guy, sweet jewels employ
Toddle your fingers up and down my chest, I'm your toy
Electric, your fingers inside my core, and prick me more
Sensual are the nature of sex, rays of fantasy you implore

Handsome and comely like an angel on wings
Make ready my colours, my rainbow on wind
Twinkle my stars, please entice me dear babe
Arouses hot, savour me to the tingle of your pain

Lie me down lover, on this silk shade of sheets
Sparkle me with bubbles, and feed me with heat
Delicate, slowly insert your cock inside my sweet
Dance me with sex; waver in thoughts, my juices are wet

By Lisa Clark

Sexual Zest

Lust so delicate, the fire they share
Whispers so soft, elegance, passions endear
Surrounding her raptures, caught in ecstasy
Favoring her needs, so precious in fantasy

Her nipple are ripe, they prosper his taste
Areolas so tender so beautiful they glaze
He nipped on her flesh so provocatively blest
He suck her wet tongue, joy put me to the test

My fingers do crawl, they lavish and played
Inside her core, they calmly did obeyed
Her tender moans softly bore his name
She's breathless in waves, this shivering dame

Her parted thighs sure nested his world
Her pleasure of lux, his desires they burn
He plucked her flavored, sweet joy they bring
Her heat is wet, fluids flowing like spring

He mastered her mind, encirclement of love
His dildo prepared, in heat he did shove
Hot pacing of pleasures, he throbbed forthwith
Bewildered his pulses, each moment felt crisp

Tardiness of sweet rhythms, tranquil my tides
She raked in his juices like water in bliss
She pennied his thought, this maiden of love
Her blessing he jeered, she's pretty as a dove

By Lisa Clark

Sexual Bon

Creamy and sexual wicked forte bain
Tasting austere, precious sweet pain
Naughty, beautiful hard on with paste
Touching my depths of nestered zest

Daring delights, so buttery and wet
Crave me, knight me in your peppered net
Melt me, take me to the limits on high
Bliss me, kiss me, on clouds in the sky

Budding my nipples sugary for you
Whipped cream of juices ever so true
Wild me, engrave me in your party of desires
Nudge me, budge me in the jades of your fire

My dancing prince, my secrets of time
Has wandered the oceans and flew in the each time
He touched my lips with each dancing rhyme
His heart rend of passions tore open my thighs

His hard warm dick pressed on my peach
I felt his sweet ripples filled in my reach
Adorn from his pleasure, delicious nectar
He shoved it in precious, my eyes met the stars

Slippery and slick, he grind me with fuck
Holding me tightly each daring he tucked
Loving each minute I know I am blest
His true words of purpose, his true words of silk

By Lisa Clark

Skin Dipper

Touching the soft contours of my core
Tasting hot pleasures I'm craving for more
Twiggle your tongue in my fiery desires
Spin my fantasies to your passion treasures

Touch me entirely, the nature being of my flesh
Make ready your feast to comfort your sexuality
Grant me the perfection of your fine pleasures
Fill me delicately; purge me with your hot chocolate

Burn me with the heat of your erotic so naughty
Precious is your libido this tantalizing my dreams
Luscious and lewd, provocative and passionate
You are truly blest by cupid dart of naked love

You make me hot and streaming, wild and wicked
Each rhythmical strides pace to gratify my wet ripples
Each metaphoric twist rang my high notes
Build my zeal to the corners of your sensual concepts

I am like a feather's sprig, softly and swaying
So delightful with satisfaction and peaceful with calm
You mystically enrapture the mysteries of my thoughts
Passions enfolding in the strength of your heat

By Lisa Clark

Slippery Lollipop

Sweet and sultry, naughty and nude
Delicious and tasty, ecstactical mood
I lay with precious silk by my side
I lay with tenderness awaiting his stride

The room is dark, the bright moon shone
The air is peaceful as shadows cast round
I ponder my thought I pondered my care
I whispered his name, his essence drew near

An essence of feeling electrifies the air
An aroma of him so tingled my fears
He touched my thighs, I froze with zest
He twinkled his fingers across my chest

He declines his head and chewed my lips
I felt each ripples, so nurtured his bits
He sucked my nipples, he fondled my butt
I closed my eyes so ready to fuck

His cock stood stiff so wet and ready
He open my legs redeemed and steady
My sapling was drooling swell and heavy
His hot dick dares dangles and begging

He fucked me wild from sense to crazed
I received his passions endorsed ablaze
We mentor each position from start to finish
We took turns in twineing without a blemish

The moon so smiled as it fed my face
His muscles firm he grips each pace
Gyrated moments build ease throb
He body flush down his juices if cum

By Lisa Clark

Stolen Secrets

I dream of days my passions endorsed
I dream of desired emblemed so remote
I captured my thoughts in this realm so wide
I blend each moment with regards so high

He held my essence swifts my soul
He kissed my paths here tread so close
In the cool dew morn my dearest of rose
I listened attentive to his prism of praise
His tenders of words caress their grace

His eyes seem to pave like dark purple beads
Sings its dark message ought whispers the breeze
I studied each pairs, I dare kept my peace
A message redeeming that read in each reed
Message detriments its passion here need

His passion grew daring the beast to unleash
I endorsed his charms, I calm his teals
He secretly grapple my caramel breasts
He tasted with care so tasky was his test
His warm blooded fingers fondled my rest

Softly and smoothly he part my thighs
Silky with softness, he strike my mare high
He shoved his cock in my bare naughty
And then came the prism of my colorful ecstasy
His beast rode my rhythms in my blue fantasy

He sexual gasps while fucking my thrill
His tendons pact tender and whisper in shrill
Sweet nothings I listens to his true soft voice
Sweet nothings care worthings my verve hence poised
He propelled each notion the concepts undone

The language his body rhythmical told
A language so spoken of passion so bold
I felt his energy connected with mine
A spiritual bondness it fuses our time
I nurtured his prospered so dearly sublime

Unleashed, exploding echoes his beams
His body in shivers, eclipses its redeems
He's caught in sweet panic a crazy fuck jet
His splash like dew drops the sheets became wet
The preen scene of mystics hence dandle our quest

By Lisa Clark

Strawberry Lollipop

She toy with a strawberry lollipop
Sucked it; she licked its flavour contents
It felt juicy, wet, warm and sticky
The aromatic scent of her lollipop
Melting buttery on her tongue
Tasting soft as a strawberry fruit

Doth she toyed with this lollipop
she thought of his awesome essence
Feeling the strength of his ever grand
His huge, heavy cock inside her mouth
This caramel sweet, sexual toy of her
She sucked, and licked the dribbles of juice

Sexual delight.......sated and wet
His dick is stiff, warm with juices
You create shivers of ripples up her spine
Savouring his blend and so delicious
Wetting her lips with your sweet hot splash

By Lisa Clark

Unchained Love

She tasted all his flames laced with sweet romantic leisure
A romance of a lifetime that would bond them both forever
A wonderful land of ecstasy, a perfect hidden treasure
A paradise of unveiled love, a chamber of pure passion

Two lovers intertwine, scenes of rapture to behold
A garden full of rainbow, it's like heaven untold
A pleasant delight, a melodious velvet bliss
He enchants his lover, what a seasonal twist

A room full of jewels, a portal of pure mystics
She receive her lord in the realms so angelic
She whispers his name, so delicate she swing
As he pushes and slithers, he listens as she sing

What perfect hidden treasure the lovers do provoke
Their swindling of passion, compelling each stroke
Unchained is their ecstasy, untangle is their toy
Unending is their mystery, undying is their joy

By Lisa Clark

Velvet Glow

I love you with a sense because I sense the
language of the soul
I love you silently because silence is the
language of minds
I love you with whispers because whispering is
the language of the heart
I love you by touch because touch
is language of the body
I love you by smiling because smiling is the
language of the lips
I love you with tears because tears are
language of the eyes
I love you in silence because silence is the
language of the night

I love you in summer because summer is the
season of warmth
I love in autumn because autumn is the
season of sadness
I love you very much because winter is the
season of joy
I love you in spring because spring is the
season for hope
I love you with fire because fire is the
language of chemistry
I love you with whiteness of snow because it is the
language of purity
I love you quietly because quiet is the
language of honesty
I love you with sacrifice because sacrifice is the
language fulfilled
I love you by my pen because my pen is the
language of love
I love you in all the languages of the world because you are the
language of love

by Lisa Clark

Wet Passions

Touch the soft contours of my core
Taste the pleasure of my hot springs
Twiggle your tongue inside my fire
Spin my fantasies to your treasure of desire

Touch me entirely, the nature of being of my flesh
Make ready your feast to comfort your sexuality
Grant me the perfection of your fine pleasure
Fill me sexually; purge me with your warm dick

Burn me with the heat of your erotic so naughty
Precious is your libido so craving my dreams
Luscious and lewd, provocative and passionate
Your are blest by cupid's dart of naked love

Your make me hot, steaming, wild and wicked
Each rhythmical strides pace to gratify my ripples
Each metaphoric twist ring my high symphony
O' build my zeal to the corners of your sensual concepts

I'm like a dancing feather, softly and swaying
So delightful with satisfaction and serenity
You mystically enraptured my thoughts
Passions enfolding the strength of your heat

By Lisa Clark

Wet Sex

Taste my bubbles, taste my blends
Taste my flavour that never ends
Feel my sweetness, feel my grace
Savoir the berries, savoir the crave

Lick my body, and lick my chest
Lick each moment, nurture each fest
Kissing my lips, my lover, my babe
Take me to neverland, take me away

Twiggle my chemistry twiggle my clit
Twiggle me sexual with your warm dick
Nesting your pressure, peaking you high
Blessing each fester, raking you nigh

Now you're ready delicious for love
Now you are ready for some peppered fuck
Supple and wild, wet is yours glans
As you shove your cock inside my sap

This fuck feast fete, here we dot expound
This slippery tight fuck is well cast bound
You took me in caramel toffee, sweet fantasy
You created rainbows in a world of ecstasy

What prince are so you dominantly bless
It knows no bounds and praises are best
You held my hand so soft and gentle
You flavour this boon ere you are subtle

By Lisa Clark